Once Upon A Time...

Once Upon A Time....

Celebrating the Magic of Children's books
in honor of the Twentieth Anniversary of
READING IS FUNDAMENTAL

G·P·Putnam's Sons
New York

Copyright Acknowledgments

Atheneum Publishers for the text and illustrations by Ashley Bryan. Text copyright © 1985 by Ashley Bryan. Illustration copyright © 1976 by Ashley Bryan, from *The Adventures of Aku*. Used by permission of Atheneum Publishers.

Dial Books for Young Readers for the use of the illustration from *Ralph's Secret Weapon* by Steven Kellogg. Copyright © 1983 by Steven Kellogg. Used by permission of Dial Books for Young Readers.

Harper & Row, Publishers, Inc., for text on unnumbered p. 5 ("Little Red Riding Hood") from *Self-Portrait* written and illustrated by Trina Schart Hyman. Copyright © 1981 by Trina Schart Hyman. Reprinted by permission of Harper & Row, Publishers, Inc.

Harper & Row, Publishers, Inc., for text and art on pages 20-21 from *Where the Sidewalk Ends* by Shel Silverstein. Copyright © 1974 by Snake Eye Music, Inc. Reprinted by permission of Harper & Row, Publishers, Inc.

Holiday House for the illustration from *Little Red Riding Hood* by Trina Schart Hyman. © 1983 by Trina Schart Hyman. Reprinted by permission of Holiday House.

Lothrop, Lee & Shepard Books for the excerpt from *Eyes of Darkness*. © 1985 by Jamake Highwater. By permission of Lothrop, Lee & Shephard Books (a Division of William Morrow & Co., Inc.)

Macmillan Publishing Company for excerpts from *The Voyage of the Dawn Treader* by C. S. Lewis. Copyright 1952 C. S. Lewis Pte, Ltd., copyright renewed 1980. Reprinted by permission of Macmillan Publishing Company.

William Morrow & Co., Inc., for the excerpt from *Ramona the Brave*, used by permission of William Morrow & Co., Inc., © 1975 by Beverly Cleary.

William Morrow & Co., Inc., for the illustrations from *Ramona the Brave* by Beverly Cleary. Illustrations by Alan Tiegreen © 1975 William Morrow & Co., Inc.

Philomel Books for the use of the illustration from *When The Sun Rose* by Barbara Helen Berger. Copyright © 1986 by Barbara Helen Berger. Reprinted by permission of Philomel Books, a division of The Putnam Young Readers Group.

Philomel Books for use of the illustration from *Rosemary for Remembrance* by Tasha Tudor. Copyright © 1981 by Tasha Tudor. Reprinted by permission of Philomel Books, a division of The Putnam Young Readers Group.

Random House, Inc., for the text and illustration from *I Can Read With My Eyes Shut* by Dr. Seuss. Copyright © 1978 by Dr. Seuss and A. S. Geisel. Reprinted by permission of Random House, Inc.

Reading Is Fundamental, Inc., for use of the illustration by Maurice Sendak. Copyright © 1979 by Reading Is Fundamental, Inc.; reprinted by permission of RIF, Inc.

Viking Penguin for use of the illustration from *Madeline* by Ludwig Bemelmans. Copyright © 1939 by Ludwig Bemelmans. Copyright renewed 1967 by Madeline Bemelmans & Barbara Bemelmans Marciano. Reprinted by permission of Viking Penguin.

Library of Congress Cataloging-in-Publication Data
Once upon a time. Summary: An illustrated collection of true and fictional anecdotes,
stories, and reminiscences by well-known children's authors and illustrators about books
and the experience of reading.   1. Children–Books and reading.   2. Authors, American–
20th century–Books and reading.   3. Illustrators–United States–Books and reading.
4. Children's literature–Appreciation–United States. 5. Books and reading–United States.
[1. Books and reading.   2. Reading.   3. Authors, American.   4. Illustrators]
I. Reading is fundamental, inc.   Z1037.A1053   1986   028.5'5   86-18715
ISBN 0-399-21369-4   ISBN 0-399-21370-8 (pbk.)

To readers of all ages,
especially those
who share their love of reading
with children

Contents

We would like to give very special thanks to the following contributors whose generosity helped make this book possible:

Arcata Graphics/Kingsport

Dilys Evans Fine Illustration

Expertype, Inc.

Fisher Composition, Inc.

Jeanyee Wong for her calligraphy

Jellybean Photographic Labs

Scranton Label, Inc.

Willmann Paper Company/Potlatch Corporation

Atheneum Publishers; Dial Books for Young Readers; Federated Lithographers-Printers, Inc.; Harper & Row, Publishers; Holiday House; Lothrop, Lee & Shepard Books; Macmillan Publishing Co.; William Morrow & Co., Inc.; Offset Printing Van Den Bossche; Philomel Books; Random House, Inc.; RIF, Inc.; Viking Penguin; Worzalla Publishing Co. for granting us permission to reprint previously published pieces and for supplying duplicate film

Acknowledgments

Reading Is Fundamental is honored that so many of the most distinguished contributors to contemporary children's literature have shared their special talents to create this unique tribute to Reading Is Fundamental (RIF). We extend our sincerest thanks to each of the authors and artists whose work appears in these pages.

And we are deeply grateful to the Putnam Young Readers Group for their imaginative generosity. In celebrating RIF's twentieth anniversary with the publication of *Once Upon A Time,* Putnam has produced what should become a classic that both children and adults will enjoy for years to come.

Our heartfelt thanks to all who were involved in the creation and production of this special book, especially to Tomie dePaola who sparked its beginning, and to Margaret Frith, editor and fairy godmother who made it happen. Special thanks to Nanette Stevenson for her creative art direction, and to Victoria Rock, editor, for her devoted attention to every detail. And our sincere appreciation goes to the people in the Putnam Art, Production, Marketing, and Sales departments, and to all of the suppliers and others who generously donated their services to making *Once Upon a Time* a beautiful reality, we thank you.

In honoring Reading Is Fundamental, this book is also a tribute to the hundreds of thousands of RIF volunteers who have made it possible for millions of young people throughout the nation to have books of their own and to experience the joy of reading.

RIF

Introduction

Jim Trelease

This is a book of beginnings. That alone makes it a wonderful book because most people feel beginnings are always more exciting and hopeful than endings. I much prefer the beginning of summer, the opening day of baseball season, the start of a party, or the first licks of a lollypop to the *last* of those things.

It is also appropriate for this book to mark the twentieth anniversary of RIF—Reading Is Fundamental—an organization dedicated to bringing good books into the permanent possession of children throughout America. RIF is one of a kind and so is this book. I know of no other book for children quite like it.

In stories and pictures, an assortment of children who grew up to become authors and artists reach back to their childhoods and share their feelings about the special relationship they had with books.

I write "special" relationship to distinguish it from simply learning how to read. Most children eventually learn to read but, sadly, many miss out on the specialness of books. As you will read here, sometimes that experience begins on a parent's lap, other times in the neighborhood library. It can happen in the shade of a tree or, as one artist describes, deep beneath the covers of his bed.

You'll read how the feeling between a young reader and the book can be so special it provoked one author to steal her favorite library book and hide it for fear it was the only copy in the whole world. It is a specialness that is often filled with secrets—secret people, places and feelings—that last a lifetime. Many of these authors and artists are expressing their childhood feelings, yet the memories are still as fresh to them as though they happened only yesterday.

These memories are special largely because they are *first* memories of reading. A famous editor and a great reader, Clifton Fadiman, once made an interesting observation about first memories. He recalled the first book he ever read, a farm story called *The Overall Boys.* It's still a favorite of his, seventy years and tens of thousands of books later. Why? Because it was the first. After that he became an avid reader, always looking for a book as good as *The Overall Boys.* He claims he's never found one better because that first great taste of the reading world can never be equaled. "One's first book, kiss, home run, is always the best," he once wrote.

When I ask children, "Why should we read?" they usually answer, "To find the answers."

"But the answers to *what?*" I ask next. That usually stumps them for a bit. Then someone will say, "Questions."

"Ahaa!" I respond. "And do you know the most important questions of all? They've interviewed people all over the world and these seem to be the two most important and often asked questions: Who am I? and Why am I? In other words, what kind of a person am I? Why am I here in this world? How is my *own* story going to turn out? What's my plot?"

Books give us some of the clues we need to answer those questions. Sometimes the clue is buried in a character we meet in a story, a trait we might like or dislike.

While I cannot read the minds of the people who wrote and illustrated this book, I do suspect there is a great hopefulness there. They create their books with the trust there will be someone—a parent or a teacher, a librarian, even an older sibling—someone who will act as an intermediary between the author and the child. After all, people are never born wanting to read, any more than they are born wanting to play baseball or the piano. So count among the needs of the world those special people who help children discover the meaning behind those strange marks that add up to an alphabet, who thankfully let children know there is more to reading than workbook pages.

For it is today's children who are so touched by the joy of reading who in turn will share it with another generation years from now, when they themselves become parents or teachers or maybe even authors. And the more such shared beginnings, the less likely the joy of reading will ever end.

Once Upon A Time...

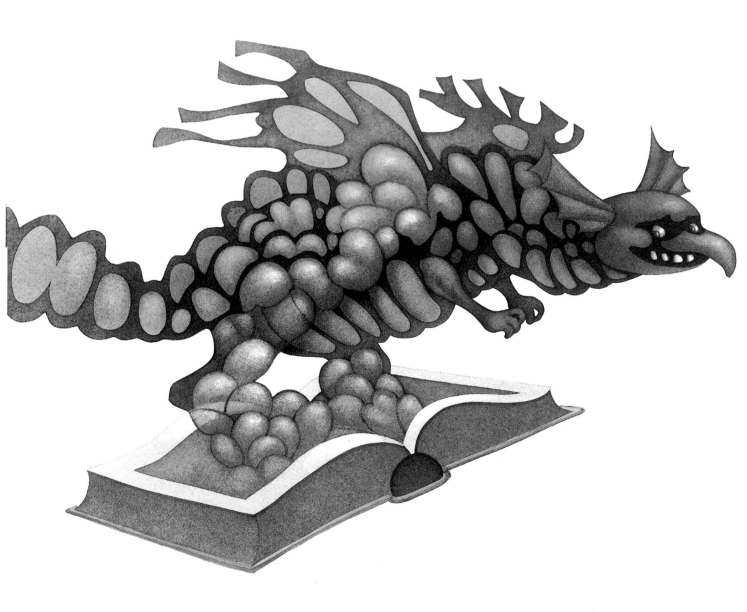

I Met a Dragon Face to Face

Jack Prelutsky

I met a dragon face to face
the year when I was ten,
I took a trip to outer space,
I braved a pirates' den,
I wrestled with a wicked troll,
and fought a great white shark,
I trailed a rabbit down a hole,
I hunted for a snark.

I stowed aboard a submarine,
I opened magic doors,
I traveled in a time machine,
and searched for dinosaurs,
I climbed atop a giant's head,
I found a pot of gold,
I did all this in books I read
when I was ten years old.

The Secret Life of
Katherine Clements Womeldorf

Katherine Paterson

Yes, I had a long and peculiar name that I was not absolutely sure how to spell until I was nearly through the third grade. This was, perhaps, one reason why my teachers suspected that I was not very bright. I also wore strange, hand-me-down clothes and spoke with a foreign accent, which may help explain my shortage of friends in those early years. At home I took out my unhappiness with displays of temper and a lack of responsibility which made my grandmother constantly assure my harassed mother that I would come to no good end.

My grandmother might have been right except for one thing. I had a secret life, a life peopled with wonderful friends who understood me and who made me feel smart and loveable. You might complain that my "secret life" wasn't a real life at all. It was only in my imagination. Maybe so. But it was real enough to make those years bearable, and powerful enough to make my public self begin to grow toward the private self of my dreams.

At school my teachers were listening to me stumble through the Dick and Jane readers. They would have been amazed to know about my secret life in which I was feasting on great fat books with many-syllabled words I've never learned how to pronounce properly.

The chief book I remember from those years was *The Secret Garden* by Frances Hodgson Burnett. Mary was my best friend in my secret life. She had come from India rather than China, but she was just as bad-tempered and even less popular than I. And then she made wonderful discoveries at the great dark house where she had been sent to live—a mysterious cry in the night, a boy who could enchant animals and bring flowers from the barren earth, and, best of all, a secret garden.

The secret garden was like my secret life, and Mary and Dickon and Colin became my friends there. They were joined by Kate, the spoiled Hungarian tomboy in *The Good Master,* Jo from *Little Women* (I didn't invite her sisters), a wonderful mouse named Amos who taught Benjamin Franklin all he ever knew (from *Ben and Me* by Robert Lawson), and many other unappreciated misfits and little guys who showed everyone, by golly, and who, though I didn't fully understand it at the time, became more human and loving in the process.

In his autobiography, Frederick Douglass tells how his master caught his mistress teaching him the alphabet. The master was enraged. Not only was it against the law to teach a slave to read, but it would make him unmanageable and unfit to be a slave. "From that moment," Douglass says, "I understood the pathway from slavery to freedom. Whilst I was saddened by the thought of losing the aid of my kind mistress, I was gladdened by the invaluable instruction which, by the merest accident, I gained from my master. Though conscious of the difficulty of learning without a teacher, I set out with high hope, and a fixed purpose, at whatever cost of trouble, to learn how to read. . . ."

Although the difficulties of my childhood cannot be compared to those Douglass endured, I too learned that reading can be a road to freedom or a key to a secret garden, which, if tended, will transform all of life.

IT WAS MY SECRET PLACE-
  DOWN AT THE FOOT
  OF MY BED-
  UNDER THE COVERS.

IT WAS VERY WHITE.

I WENT THERE
  WITH A BOOK, A FLASHLIGHT,
  AND THE SPECIAL PENCIL
  THAT MY GRANDFATHER GAVE ME,

TO READ
AND TO DRAW PICTURES
ON ALL THAT WHITE.

IT WAS MY SECRET PLACE
FOR ABOUT A WEEK-

UNTIL MY MOTHER CAME
  TO CHANGE THE SHEETS.

♥ DEPAOLA '86 · FOR R.I.F.

M. B. Goffstein

W. Somerset Maugham wrote that people aren't always born at home.

We can see the world through books, and the books will be our tents.

Friends for Life

Judy Blume

When I was small my mother took me to the public library in Elizabeth, New Jersey, where I would sit on the floor and browse among the books. I not only liked the pictures and the stories, but also the feel and the smell of the books themselves. My favorite book was *Madeline* by Ludwig Bemelmans. I loved that book! I loved it so much that I hid it in my kitchen toy-drawer so my mother wouldn't be able to return it to the library. Even after the overdue notices came I didn't tell my mother where the book was. If only I had asked, I'm sure she would have bought me my own copy, but I didn't know then that was a possibility. I thought the copy I had hidden was the only copy in the whole world. I knew it was wrong to hide the book, but there was no way I was going to part with *Madeline.* I memorized the words in the book, and though I couldn't really read, I pretended that I could.

When I did learn to read I was very proud. Not only could I read *Madeline,* but I could read the back of the cereal box, just like my older brother. When I visited my aunt and uncle I was allowed to take their beautifully illustrated copy of *Mother Goose* from the bookshelf—as long as I washed my hands first—and I would read the nursery rhymes on my own. In school we were divided into reading groups with bird names. I was a bluejay in first grade and a robin in second. But the stories in our readers about Dick and Jane and Spot weren't nearly as much fun as the stories in the books I chose myself. I loved getting into bed at night with a favorite book and reading until my father said it was time to put out my light.

I read all the Oz books, the Nancy Drew mysteries, and the Betsy–Tacy books by Maud Hart Lovelace. When I was older, in junior high, I discovered the books on my parents' bookshelves. No one ever told me what books I could read or what books I couldn't. On my own I found Salinger's *Catcher in the Rye,* Bellow's *The Adventures of Augie March* and Ayn Rand's *The Fountainhead.* I still read and reread these authors. Books opened up a whole new world to me. Through them I discovered new ideas, traveled to new places, and met new people. Books helped me learn to understand other people and they taught me a lot about myself.

It's more than forty years since I hid that copy of *Madeline,* and I've never done that again, but I can still recite the story by heart. And when my daughter was born, *Madeline* was the first book I bought for her. Betsy and Tacy are still alive in my mind, and when I close my eyes I can picture them on a summer day as they call on their neighbor Tib. Some books you never forget. Some characters become your friends for life.

I loved getting lost in books when I was young. I still do!

Margot Tomes

Peter Pan, the Pilgrims, a Pirate and a Cat

Jean Fritz

When I was young, reading books was always a chance for me to go somewhere else. (It still is.) I went to England with Mother Goose so much as a little girl that when I really and truly did go when I was a grown-up, I felt right at home. Banbury Cross? Of course. And St. Ives. I haven't been to Switzerland yet, but when I go, I'll recognize it, all right. I've walked up and down mountain paths with Heidi; I've seen those meadows of wildflowers.

Yet for some reason there were a few books that didn't take me away from home at all. Instead the characters in those books walked into my house in Hankow, China, and settled down to live with me. In whatever room I happened to be when I first met them, that's where they generally stayed.

It was a cold winter day when my mother read me "The Cat Who Walked by Himself," one of Kipling's *Just So Stories.* We were sitting in the dining room before the fireplace to keep warm, and as my mother read, the French doors between the dining room and the porch opened noiselessly, and out of the wet wild woods somewhere far beyond the porch came The Cat Who Walked by Himself. Swishing his tail, he announced that he was The Cat Who Walked by Himself and all places were alike to him. But I knew he wanted to get warm and I wasn't surprised when he went straight to the fireplace, curled up on the hearth, and went to sleep. And he's been there ever since. No matter how many times I read the story, no matter how many times I watch him walking alone through the wet wild woods, he always ends up on the hearth in that first house of mine.

As for the Pilgrims, I knew very well that John and Priscilla Alden, Miles

Standish and the rest lived in Plymouth, Massachusetts, and you would think I would have left them there. But no. In the living room of that same house my father read me Longfellow's *The Courtship of Miles Standish,* the only book I ever remember him reading to me. I sat on his lap as he read and I was so happy I guess I didn't want to risk the trip to Plymouth. So I simply brought the Pilgrims into the room with us. Of course, to anyone else they might have seemed out of place, plunked down in the middle of China with the *Mayflower* anchored a few blocks away in the Yangtze River. But not to me. They were my friends, and to this day I picture them settling down in the New World but doing it in our living room in China.

I was sick a lot in my childhood. Once I had a bad ear infection and had to stay in bed for a couple of weeks. My mother bought me a copy of *Peter Pan,* and that's when he moved into the house, flying through the window of my blue bedroom, perching on my white bedstead. I never could quite picture Never Never Land so I had no desire to go there. Moreover, I didn't much like Wendy taking care of Peter, being such a good little housewife, so I ignored her. It was Peter who came alone to visit me after my mother turned out my light at night. I'd imagine a little swishing sound at the window and in Peter would fly. It didn't take me long to learn to fly too, and until I got sleepy, we'd zoom out of the window and fly together all over Hankow. Indeed, I can't imagine him anyplace else.

Bluebeard was a character who also seemed very real to me. Too real, actually. Sometimes I'd wish I had never met him and I certainly didn't want to go where he was—nor did I want him hanging around my house. Still, I didn't seem to have a choice: he was there. The best thing I could do was to put him out of the way in the attic. There were three rooms in the attic. I put him and all his wives in the corner of one room. I didn't take any chances—I chained them there. Then I shut the door of the room and never went in there again. But one day my cat had kittens and my father, carrying them all in a box to the attic, started to open Bluebeard's door. Well, I loved those kittens; I wasn't going to allow that. I put up such a fuss that he finally put them in another room, although he couldn't understand why I was so upset.

Recently I went back to China for the first time since I'd left it as a girl. I found my old house, knocked on the door, introduced myself to the people who live there now, and was invited in for tea. Of course the house was furnished very differently and there were more people living in it. But it didn't seem strange to me. Underneath the life that was going on there, I could still feel the layer that I had lived in. I could feel myself as a little girl sharing those very rooms with my mother and father and my amah, Lin Nai Nai, and our servants and friends. And yes, The Cat Who Walked by Himself was just where I'd left him. And the Pilgrims. Peter Pan too. I don't know about Bluebeard. I didn't go up to the attic and if I had, you can be sure I wouldn't have opened his door.

Picture People

Myra Cohn Livingston

I like to peek
   inside a book
   where all the picture people look.

I like to peek
   at them and see
   if they are peeking back at me.

Little Red Riding Hood

Trina Schart Hyman

I was a really strange little kid. I was born terrified of anything and every-thing that moved or spoke. I was afraid of people, especially. All people—kids my own age, all grown-ups, even my own family. Dogs (until my parents bought me a puppy of my own), horses, trees, grass, cars, streets. I was afraid of the stars and the wind. Who knows why?

My mother is a beautiful woman with red hair and the piercing blue gaze of a hawk. She never seemed afraid of anyone or anything. It was she who gave me the courage to draw and a love of books. She read to me from the time I was a baby, and once, when I was three or four and she was reading my favorite story, the words on the page, her spoken words, and the scenes in my head fell together in a blinding flash. I could read!

The story was "Little Red Riding Hood," and it was so much a part of me that I actually became Little Red Riding Hood. My mother sewed me a red satin cape with a hood that I wore almost every day, and on those days, she would make me a "basket of goodies" to take to my grandmother's house. (My only grandmother lived in Rhode Island, three hundred miles away, but that didn't matter.) I'd take the basket and carefully negotiate the backyard, "going to Grandmother's house." My dog, Tippy, was the wolf. Whenever we met, which in a small backyard had to be fairly often, there was an intense confrontation. My father was the woodsman, and I greeted him when he came home each day with relief and joy.

I was Red Riding Hood for a year or more. I think it's a great tribute to my mother that she never gave up and took me to a psychiatrist, and if she ever worried, she has never let me know.

from Eyes of Darkness

Jamake Highwater

Whenever the Indians of the Plains went on the warpath, it was their custom to test the young warriors, putting them through many ordeals before they ever came face to face with the enemies. And so it happened that Yesa and his brother, Chatanna, were put to the test by their elders. When they were near a hostile Indian camp, the brothers were selected to go after the water, though the creek was dangerously close to the enemies.

Yesa was ready for the challenge. Together with Chatanna, he picked his way through the dark woods, dipped the pail into the water as quickly and as quietly as possible, and then hurried back to camp. The two brothers' hearts leaped at every crackling twig, every hoot of the owls, until at last they reached the tipi of their uncle.

Mysterious Medicine smiled proudly at both of them, and they breathed a sigh of relief as they turned to join the men around the fire. But their uncle was not finished with their test. Slowly he turned the bucket on its side and spilled the contents on the ground.

"Yes, Yesa and Chatanna, it is true. I think you are going to be very brave men," he said as he emptied out the precious contents of the pail. "And so now you will fill the bucket a second time and show twice as much courage."

By the time the brothers returned to the encampment of their people the second time, they were so exhausted they could not eat. Chatanna slouched off to the lodge of his uncle, while Yesa returned to the tipi of his grandmother.

"Ai!" she exclaimed as she embraced him. "But do not forget. To be a warrior is good," she murmured as she led Yesa to his bed, "but to be wise and generous is also good!"

And then, as she put wood on the fire and squatted over the kettle, rocking to and fro on her heels, she gazed lovingly at her grandson. "Close your eyes, my strong-hearted child," she whispered, "and I will tell you a marvelous story. This is the tale of the *Hetunkala*—the field mice who live in the sky. Each night the mice saw the little sliver of the Moon grow larger. Yes, each night they saw the Moon hanging in the enormous black sky, growing so heavy that she began to fall. It was then, many years ago, that the mice nibbled gently upon her sides until she was small enough to rise once again . . . high into the deepest heavens! But one terrible night," Uncheedah murmured, "the *Hetunkala* nibbled too eagerly, leaving scars upon the silver Moon. And so they were hurled down to the Earth, and they lost their special place in the sky. And ever since that day, they have gathered when the Moon is full, trying to find their way back among the Stars."

The grandmother smiled and touched Yesa's black hair. "Be strong of heart . . . be patient!" she whispered as he drifted to sleep. "But above all, Yesa, learn to dream, for there is no secret and no power in a man who does not know how to dream."

The wings of birds fluttered in the moonlight. The willows grew greener. And with every gust of wind the butterflies changed places in the branches of his mind, beating their translucent wings into colors and dreams as he slept.

And then it was morning.

The Making of Dreams

Ed Young

Our summer nights were usually spent on the flat roof of the three-story house that my father designed. Against the background of crickets chirping in the starry night, my father would spin endless tales of his own to entertain our imaginations until the heat finally subsided.

The reading of the classic tales often filled the winter nights beside our big stove. Many were from Western literature drawn from my siblings' school curriculum. Some of the books included illustrations by Dulac, Pyle and Wyeth. I still hear my father's voice telling *Robinson Crusoe, The Three Musketeers, Treasure Island,* and *The Arabian Nights,* and I recall particularly my sorrow over the fate of the swallow in "The Happy Prince." I never have forgotten the images that I saw in my mind as I listened!

It wasn't until twenty-four years later, when the advertising studio where I worked closed, that I unexpectedly stumbled into picture books. It rekindled all the joy of those magical moments of the bygone days. The vivid memory of "The Master Storyteller of them all" in his Ukrainian hat and Chinese robe, sharing the riches of the world with me in those wintery nights, will remain as mine.

This Book Belongs to Me!

Arnold Lobel

From my house in Schenectady, New York, where I grew up, the long walk to the library was downhill all the way. I would return the books that I had borrowed and would quickly stock up on five new selections. Five—as I remember, that was the limit of the number of books that one could take out at a time.

Then I would begin the journey back. What I would feel, as I climbed uphill toward home with these five books, was not the anticipation of the stories and pictures that I was to pore over and enjoy, but an overwhelming feeling of absolute possession. These books were mine, all mine, and the inevitability of having to return them to the library in two weeks never entered my thoughts. I was the true owner of these pleasantly hard, rectangular objects I carried under my arm and that was that.

Schenectady, of course, is deeply inland, so I did not have cliffs and distant seas as does the cat in this picture. However, there was a large tree in my front yard and I would flop down in the shady grass. I savored my new acquisitions—savored them mostly, as I recall, because every hand-picked one of them belonged to me.

Sun and sky and bumblebee,
This book I hold belongs to me.
Grass and leaves and shady tree,
This book I read belongs to me.
Cliffs and clouds and distant sea,
This book belongs to me, to me!

Dr. Seuss

The more that you read,

the more things you will know.

The more that you learn,

the more places you'll go.

My Love Affair with the Alphabet

Natalie Babbitt

When I was in elementary school, during the last years of the 1930s and into the beginning of World War II, there were lots of things that I liked about learning to read besides the stories themselves. For one thing, we had, in the first and second grades, a big easel-like thing that stood in the front of the room and held a huge copy of our reading-lesson book. The pages turned over at the top instead of at the side, but otherwise they were exactly like the pages in our book, pictures and all, and they were made of thick, glossy paper. You got to go up front with a pointer and read out the words while you pointed to them, and everybody else would follow along in their books. I liked the feel of the pointer in my hand, and I liked tapping those shiny pages with its tip while I read out the Dick and Jane stories that we all learned on in those days.

I can remember my feeling of amazement and power when I began to recognize words in the magazines my mother and father had around the house. I had always liked looking at the pictures in those magazines, but the print had never been anything but a dense jumble of letters. And then one day I found that some of that jumble was beginning to form itself into words that I knew, words I'd learned in school. It was a little like bringing a blurry television picture into focus—suddenly things made sense. And I was hooked.

The alphabet is still a miracle to me—how those twenty-six funny shapes can group themselves in endlessly different ways to make words with end-lessly different meanings. I still play alphabet games with myself, games like trying to think of five words that are exactly the same except for the vowels, like bAg, bEg, bIg, bOg and bUg. Just by changing the vowels, you can utterly change the meaning. And another game I like is trying to find words that contain letters in alphabetical order. For instance, ABsConD and DE-FoG, and my favorite, HIJacK.

My mother and I used to play a game called Anagrams where you made words out of letters printed on small, tidy squares of thick cardboard. Every once in a while, one would drop on the floor, and Dingo, our dog, would chew it. We didn't mind so much if it was a *J* or a *Q* because those were hard letters to use, but it was bad if an *E* or an *S* got chewed. Still, we just let them dry out and used them anyway, rumpled though they were with tooth marks.

Now my daughter, Lucy, and I play Boggle whenever we're together. The letters for this game are printed on wooden cubes, and Rosie, the dog we have now, isn't much interested in them. I think dogs like the taste of paper better—Rosie always enjoys a paper napkin for a snack if she can sneak one. But whether they're printed on cardboard or wood or on the pages of a book, for me it's the same fascination over and over—those twenty-six funny shapes and the magical things they can do with each other.

Another reason why I was eager to learn to read was that I have a sister who is two years older than I am, so of course she learned first. And she was a very good reader who liked hard, heavy books. It was important to me to try to catch up with her. But it took a long time. In the beginning, when we went to the library, which was not in our elementary school but in the junior high school up the street, we got our books from different shelves. Hers were high up, while mine were on the very bottom so that I had to squat down to see what was there and make my choices.

Also, because of her constant reading, my sister had a truly amazing vocabulary at an early age. This made it possible for her to say what she said in ways that often struck me dumb. Once, playing jacks on the front porch, I impatiently reminded her that it was her turn, and she said, "I am fully cognizant of that fact." This is why Linus Van Pelt's manner of speaking in the *Peanuts* comic strip has always seemed perfectly reasonable to me. My sister talked that way too.

For us in those days, the library was not another schoolroom, as it seems to be now. It was a place you went only if you wanted to. But a lot of us wanted to. You could check out as many as ten books a week and read them at your own speed, and if you didn't like one, you didn't have to finish it. I regularly dragged home the whole ten, and it wasn't easy. They came in such a variety of shapes and sizes—square, tall, thin, fattish, large, small—and they always slipped and slid against one another. But this was part of their charm. The books my mother and father read all seemed to be exactly the same size and shape. I think I believed they all said exactly the same things inside.

Our librarian was a person I deeply admired, for she had polished the process of checking-out down to a fine little phrase of music. *Clump*—turning the book on its face. *Snap*—flinging open its back cover. *Whisk*—taking out the card from its paper pocket. *Thump*—the date stamp on the ink pad. *Thump thump*—stamping the book's card and my card. *Snick*—thrusting my card into the paper pocket. And *snap* again—flinging the book cover shut. The only thing I've ever seen since to equal it was a graceful counterman at a White Tower diner years later who could turn the scrambling of two eggs into one long fluid movement from egg carton to serving plate without a single wasted gesture.

For a long time I wanted to be a librarian and used to practice with my own books at home, checking them in and out to imaginary patrons. But I didn't have the right kind of date stamp, so I could never make the right kind of music. And anyway, an older cousin came to live with us at about that time, and she had long fingernails that clicked when she played the piano, a sound of almost equal charm to those made by my librarian. So I quit biting my fingernails and concentrated on trying to click the way my cousin did.

But I didn't stop reading. More and more I was finding the charm, the excitement, the relief of sliding into the worlds of the stories I read, of escaping my own plain, ordinary life and becoming the hero I was reading about. So while my outer world stayed predictably the same, my inner world grew wider and wider, its possibilities infinite, the choices it suggested for how I *might* live, someday, multiplying with each new story.

Each of us has to live, finally, in her own little piece of the world, doing many things in the same way day after day, seeing the same old face in the mirror. But with books added to the day, you can be quite content. With books, your inner world has no walls. And in reading—and writing—stories, you can be many different people in many different places, doing things you would never have a chance to do in ordinary life. It's amazing that those twenty-six little marks of the alphabet can arrange themselves on the pages of a book and accomplish all that. Readers are lucky—they will never be bored or lonely.

Bears for Reading

Stan and Jan Berenstain

As cubs we both remember when
reading helped us now and then:

It helped us understand
our folks—
Papa's favorite books
had jokes;
Mama loved to read
us rhymes;
Gramps and Gran
loved oldentimes.

It helped us understand
ourselves—
All kinds of books
were on our shelves:
Nature guides and
history,
Famous tales and
mystery,

Adventure, science,
How to Draw—
Reading kept us
filled with awe!

And furthermore
we both agree
It helps us
fundamentally.

from Ramona the Brave

Beverly Cleary

"Ramona, Howie's grandmother is here," called Mrs. Quimby. "We're going now."

Ramona stepped back into her closet, slid the door shut, pressed an imaginary button, and when her imaginary elevator had made its imaginary descent, stepped out onto the real first floor and faced a real problem. Her mother and father were leaving for Parents' Night.

After Ramona said hello to Howie's grandmother ("Say hello to Howie's grandmother, Ramona"), she flopped down in a chair and peeled off one end of a Band-Aid to examine her sore knee. She was disappointed when Howie's grandmother did not notice. "I don't see why you have to go to Parents' Night," Ramona said to her mother and father. "It's probably boring."

"We want to hear what Mrs. Griggs has to say," said Mrs. Quimby.

This was what worried Ramona.

"And I want to meet the famous Mr. Cardoza," said Mr. Quimby. "We've been hearing so much about him."

"Daddy, you're really going to like him," said Beezus. "Do you know what he said when I got five wrong on my math test? He said, 'Good. Now I can see what it is you don't understand.' And then he said he was there to help me understand, and he did!"

"We're going over to Howie's house after Parents' Night," said Mrs. Quimby, "but we won't be late."

Beezus made a face and said to Ramona, "That means they'll talk about their children. They always do." Ramona knew her sister spoke the truth.

Mr. Quimby smiled as he went out the door. "Don't worry. We won't reveal the family secrets."

Beezus went off to her room, eager to do her homework on the new-to-her desk. Ramona pulled off the other Band-Aid and examined her other knee. She wondered if what Mrs. Griggs was sure to say about Susan's owl would be considered a family secret. She poked her sore knee and said, "Ouch!" so Howie's grandmother could not help hearing. When Mrs. Kemp failed to ask, Why, Ramona, how did you hurt your knee? Ramona stuck the Band-Aid back in place and studied her sitter.

Mrs. Kemp, who wore glasses with purple frames, was not the sort of sitter who played games with children. When she came to sit, she sat. She was sitting on the couch knitting something out of green wool while she looked at an old movie on television, some boring thing about grown-ups who talked a lot and didn't do much of anything. Ramona liked good lively comedies with lots of children and animals and grown-ups doing silly things. Next to that she liked cat-food commercials.

Ramona picked up the evening paper from the floor beside her chair. "Well, I guess I'll read the paper," she said, showing off for Howie's grandmother. She studied the headlines, making a sort of mental buzz when she came to words she could not read. Z-z-z-z to run for z-z-z-z, she read. Z-z-z-z of z-z-z-z-ing to go up. She turned a page. Z-z-z-z to play z-z-z-z at z-z-z-z. Play what, she wondered, and with a little feeling of triumph discovered that the Z-z-z-z-s were going to play z-z-z-z-ball.

"And what is the news tonight?" asked Mrs. Kemp, her eyes on the television set.

Attention at last. "Somebody is going to play some kind of ball," answered Ramona, proud to have actually read something in the newspaper. She hoped Mrs. Kemp would say, Why, Ramona, I had no idea you were such a good reader.

"Oh, I see," said Mrs. Kemp, a remark Ramona knew grown-ups made when they were not interested in conversation with children. Ramona tried again. "I know how to set the table," she boasted.

Instead of saying, You must be a big help to your mother, Mrs. Kemp only murmured "Mm-hm" with her eyes on the television set.

Ramona said, "I have a room of my own, and tonight I'm going to sleep in it all by myself."

"That's nice," said Mrs. Kemp absently.

Ramona gave up. Mrs. Kemp did not know the right answers.

A Tender Bridge

Ashley Bryan

I cannot remember a time when I have not been drawing and painting. In elementary school I began to make books. My first books, made in kindergarten, were illustrated ABC and counting books. These one-of-a-kind "limited editions" drew rave reviews from family and friends and were given as gifts on all occasions.

One of my earliest childhood recollections is of my mother singing. She sang from one end of the day to the other. My father used to say, "Son, your mother must think she's a bird." For his part, my father loved birds. Although his earnings as a printer were modest and there were six children to support, he couldn't resist buying birds. The living rooms of our various Bronx apartments were always lined with shelves, not for books, but for birds. At one time I counted over a hundred birds in his collection. My mother would say, "If I want any attention around here, I'd have to get into a cage."

My father played a number of instruments: saxophone, guitar, and banjo, and there was always a piano in the house. With the birds trilling, my mother singing, and the general music-making that went on at home, it is only natural that I would one day do books of the songs that had special meaning for me, the Black American spirituals. When I discovered that there were no books of these beautiful religious songs for young people to grow up with, I did my two collections, *Walk Together Children* and *I'm Going to Sing*.

As a student at the Cooper Union Art School, I began a project illustrating African art. When these illustrations were to be used in a book, I began retelling African stories. I wanted to bring something of the rich oral tradition of storytelling to the spare story motifs from which I worked.

African tales are a beautiful means of linking the living Africa, past and present, to our own present. What the African sees in his world, the questions he asks, the things that he feels and imagines, have all found their way into our stories.

There is a poem by the Senegalese poet Leopold Sedar Senghor in which he unites childhood to Eden, present to past, life to death, with the line, *"Un pont de douceur les relie"* (a tender bridge connects them). That lovely phrase stays with me as I retell and illustrate African stories. I hope that my work with the African tales will be, by the very nature of storytelling, like a tender bridge reaching us across distances of time and space.

There is no Frigate like a Book
To take us Lands away
Nor any Coursers like a Page
Of prancing Poetry—
This Traverse may the poorest take
Without oppress of Toll—
How frugal is the Chariot
That bears the Human Soul.

Emily Dickinson

Tasha Tudor

This scene was painted one evening many winters past, and is true to the room in every detail. I'm glad finally to be able to explain that the object covered by the red tablecloth is a canary cage. A few people who know me have guessed what it is, as I have over twenty-four birds. I have, however, taken artistic license in making my children younger than they really were. That is one of the many, many delights of being an artist: you can depict the world as you wish.

Barbara Helen Berger

On the next page she came to a spell "for the refreshment of the spirit." The pictures were fewer here but very beautiful. And what Lucy found herself reading was more like a story than a spell. It went on for three pages and before she had read to the bottom of the page she had forgotten that she was reading at all. . . . When she looked back at the opening words of the spell, there in the middle of the writing, where she felt quite sure there had been no picture before, she found the great face of a lion, of the Lion Aslan himself, staring into hers. It was painted such a bright gold that it seemed to be coming towards her out of the page: and indeed she was never quite sure afterwards that it hadn't really moved a little.

C. S. Lewis

Worlds of My Own

Virginia Hamilton

I read quite a lot as a child. I remember playing hard, riding my bicycle, which was a red Elgin girls' bike, and reading. When I was quite young, in second and third grade, I won prizes for reading the most books in a year. I remember one prize was a large-format picture book in full color. It had colorful ducks on the cover and I was delighted with it. That was my first award! I did well in school, especially in reading, spelling, writing, and English. We read lots of poetry and memorized it, probably from sixth grade on. We had to recite in class almost every day. We read aloud from our books every day. I enjoyed reading aloud because I read very well. It pleased me to read every word correctly. I probably practiced reading out loud at home, although I don't remember. I just have the feeling that I did. Later, in high school, I entered a statewide declamation contest and I gave my memorized speech across the county and region.

In our house, Dad read the newspaper out loud to us. He subscribed to a New York magazine called *The New Yorker* and he often read things from it to my oldest sister, Nina. It was always important to me that Dad would choose one of us to read something to. It seemed to me he read the difficult stuff to my sister. I worked hard so that he would read harder material to me.

Dad read *The Crisis* magazine to us all. I don't know if Dr. Du Bois was still the editor at the time. *The Crisis* was the official publication of the NAACP and it came to the house every month. Dad would read it to us. He was always aware of what was happening among black people and black professionals. He wanted very much that we, his children, should become fine examples of our people.

My father subscribed to various magazines and newspapers. Bless him! They made the difference in our lives, in our knowing and understanding the world outside of our rural community in Ohio. I first read William Faulkner in *The Saturday Evening Post.* I read Hemingway's *The Old Man and the Sea* in *Life.* Goodness, magazines in those days had wonderful stories. I first read Flannery O'Connor and Jean Stafford in *The New Yorker.* I read Erskine Caldwell books at home. And Steinbeck in the *Post* and the Steinbeck books my father collected.

I read all of the books my brothers and sisters brought home from school—that is, the ones that had to do with literature and poetry: I had no patience for technical books, although I had a growing fondness for astronomy and geology.

My father collected good literature and I read from his collection of the works of Edgar Allan Poe. How odd it seems now that having enjoyed the Poe stories in my childhood, I would win the Edgar Allan Poe Award, known as the Edgar, given by the Mystery Writers of America, for *The House of Dies Drear* in 1968. And strange that many years later I would write a biography of Dr. W. E. B. Du Bois and an anthology of his works. Maybe it's not so strange, though, that the seemingly casual influences of childhood become profoundly important to the adult.

I read *Native Son* and *Black Boy* by Richard Wright and *The Essays of Montaigne,* which were my father's books. De Maupassant stories, Ring Lardner stories, Jack London stories. Dad said he had known London and played baseball against him. Well, you get the idea. I read whatever was handy. I was a great reader, you might say. It was a habit I got into at an early age and that is still part of my life, although as a writer I have much less time to read for fun these days.

Christmastime was a great time for books when I was a child. It was perhaps the only time my folks felt they could afford to buy me books. At Christmas I would get one large, beautiful storybook, usually with the classic tales, such as "Cinderella" and "Puss 'n' Boots," heavily and colorfully illustrated. I remember the hours I spent off in a corner with my book. I would go into another world. I couldn't have guessed that someday I would create worlds of my own.

It's Dark in Here

Shel Silverstein

I am writing these poems
From inside a lion,
And it's rather dark in here.
So please excuse the handwriting
Which may not be too clear.
But this afternoon by the lion's cage
I'm afraid I got too near.
And I'm writing these lines
From inside a lion,
And it's rather dark in here.

GEORGIANA AS A FLYING SNAIL

HOMAGE TO THE SERVE BY GEORGIANA

MIRTH

♪Reading is WONDERFUL!♪

Edward Gorey